A
COMMON
THIRST

WRITTEN BY GARY BOELHOWER
ILLUSTRATED BY SARAH BROKKE

BEAVER'S
POND
PRESS

Book design and typesetting by James Monroe Design, LLC.
Managing Editor: Laurie Buss Herrmann

ISBN 13: 978-1-64343-854-2
Library of Congress Catalog Number: 2020916664
Printed in the United States of America
First Printing: 2020
24   23   22   21   20   5   4   3   2   1

Beaver's Pond Press, Inc.
939 Seventh Street West
Saint Paul, Minnesota 55102
(952) 829-8818
www.BeaversPondPress.com

To order, visit www.BeaversPondPress.com or call 952-829-8818.
Reseller discounts available.

Contact the author at garyboelhower.com and the illustrator at sarahbrokke.com
for school visits, speaking engagements, book club discussions, freelance projects,
and interviews.

I dedicate this story to my grandkids:
Kendra, Louis, Luigi, Samelia, and Scottie.

—Gary Boelhower

To Isaac, Freya, Sam, and Ellie:
Stay curious; it will bring you both
light and love.

—Sarah Brokke

Not far from here, the land was divided into towering mountains and level plains.

Sure-footed goats ruled the mountains, where snowfall melted into streams
that rushed down the slopes, giving the goats all the water they needed.

The plains were ruled by gentle sheep.
They were never thirsty because rain fell on the plains,
making meandering creeks.

But one year, no snow fell and not a single rain cloud filled the sky.
The stream beds turned bone dry; no green shoots or grasses grew.

The thirsty, hungry goats gathered around their wise king,
who listened to their grumblings.
"Surely," he thought, "I can convince the sheep on the plains below
to share their water and food."

The sheep were thirsty and hungry too
because the meandering creeks also
had become dry as dust.

The weary sheep gathered around their wise queen,
who listened to their grumblings.
"Surely," she thought, "I can convince the goats in the
mountains to share their water and food."

As the goats journeyed,
they saw the sheep plodding across the plains toward them.

As the sheep journeyed,
they saw the goats climbing down the mountains toward them.

The sheep and the goats met in the foothills—an unfamiliar place,
neither mountain nor plain.

When the king of the goats and the queen of
the sheep approached each other,
their scrawny bodies, dusty coats, and sad eyes
made clear neither had water or food.

A full moon cast an eerie light over the barren land. Feeling fear and mistrust, the sheep and the goats made separate camps.

"The sheep have nothing to offer us," the king said. "Let's create a safe circle and rest. We will decide what to do in the morning."

"The goats are just as hungry and thirsty as we are," said the queen.
"Let's flock close together and rest.
Tomorrow we will decide what to do."

But the young sheep and the young goats
could not sleep in the bright moonlight.

Fascinated with the foothills,
the kids and the lambs were eager to explore.

As they wandered the lambs and the kids came face to face.
At first they were afraid but then they started to speak.

The youngest lamb asked, "How do you climb on the slippery rocks
so high in the mountains?"

And the youngest kid asked,
"Doesn't your wool get heavy in the rain?"

The lambs and the kids talked and wandered late into the night until they found a cave where they could rest. Inside, moonlight shone through a crack.

As the youngest kid walked toward the light, he heard a faint gurgling, bubbling sound. Suddenly, his hoof slipped into a crevice and made a most wonderful splash. "Water!" the lambs and the kids shouted.

The older goats and sheep came running
and quickly separated the young ones.

"This is our water!" bellowed the king of the goats.
"It gurgles at the foot of the mountains,
and we rule the mountains."

"No," insisted the queen of the sheep,
"this is our water! It bubbles at the
edge of the plains and belongs to
the creatures of the plains."

The king and the queen argued for hours
as the sun rose in the sky.

Suddenly, the youngest kid collapsed.
The king of the goats declared, "We will protect
our youngest kid so he may drink."

In a weak but clear voice, the youngest kid said,
"I won't drink this water unless it is shared by us
all. We all have stories and dreams and thirst."

The king and the queen knew in their hearts
the young goat spoke the truth.
They guided the kids and lambs to drink
the gurgling, bubbling water together.

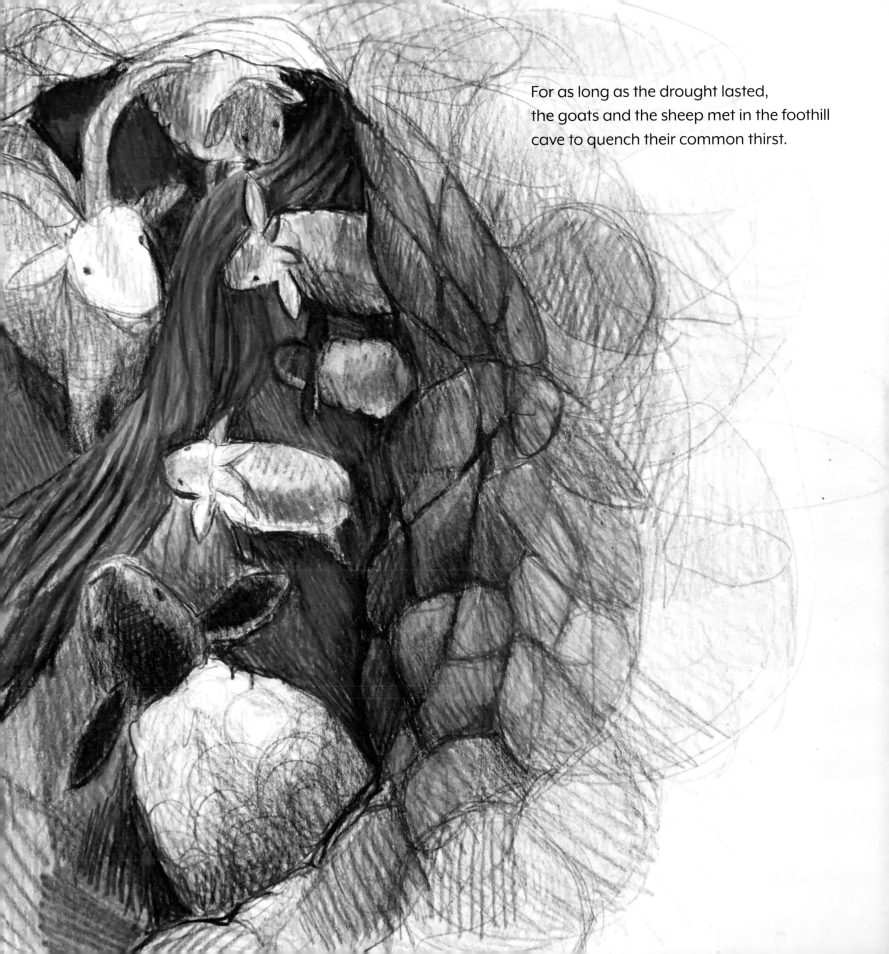

For as long as the drought lasted,
the goats and the sheep met in the foothill
cave to quench their common thirst.

At last, after several long, dry weeks,
clouds gathered over the mountains
and rain fell on the high ridges.

Water ran down the mountains
and into the valley, bringing life
to the slopes and plains again.

As the sheep and goats prepared to journey homeward, they agreed to gather in the foothills every year to always remember their common thirst, their common life.